ELSA, HENRY AND THE MOANING MOON

Written and illustrated
by Suki Baynton

This book was written and designed for my niece and nephew, Elsa and Henry and we all hope you love it.

"I'm not tired!"
Henry cried out next door.

"I'm giving you 5 minutes and
then it's lights out."
Daddy said from the landing.

Elsa sighed and turned her tablet volume up a bit
to drown her brothers moaning out.
She was on her last episode before bed and she
 wanted to enjoy it.

"But the stars aren't even out!"
Henry called out.

"3 minutes."
Daddy counted.

Elsa heard her dad turn Henry's light off followed by Henry stomping around his room.

"You too Elsa, night night."
Daddy said through her door.

She yawned and switched her tablet off.
"Night night daddy."

Elsa climbed into bed but a few minutes later heard someone tapping on her door.

"Elsa!"
Henry hissed.

"Go to bed Henry."
She said and snuggled in to her blanket.

Her door creaked open and a little head peeked in.

"Go away!" Elsa grumbled loudly.

"I can't sleep.." Henry whined.

"You're not trying." Elsa answered without opening her eyes.

"I did! Honest!" Henry said dramatically.

"But the moon and stars aren't out so it's not really night time, so I can't get tired." He rambled on.

Elsa tried to ignore him, hoping he would go away but...

Before she could hide under her blanket, Henry pounced on the bed with his space torch to show her.

"Look Elsa, look!"

He said excitedly.

"Someone has stolen the moon and stars!"

"See? No stars. No moon!"

Henry said triumphantly.

Elsa opened her eyes to look.

"Oh no, you're right. Where have they all gone?!"

Elsa said, a little worried.

"I don't know, but how am I meant to fall asleep without them?"

Henry asked.

"Well, we're going to have to investigate Henry!"

Elsa announced excitedly.

"How? We don't have a space rocket."

Henry said.

"Then we will have to build one."

Elsa grinned.

"We can't build a rocket, we're just children."
Henry said.

"Watch me." Said a very determined Elsa.

She finished her plans, gathered some bits from the house and then they crept downstairs and out to daddy's shed.

"Seats."   "Check."

"Mummy's computer."   "Check."

"Controls."   "Check."

"OK let's go!" Elsa said.

"Elsa it's amazing!" Henry bounced.

"I know." Elsa grinned.

"Now let's investigate!"

They both shouted excitedly and jumped in the rocket.

Neither of them noticed Buzz appear in the shed, give a little meow and hop on the rocket too... oops!

"3... 2... 1... Blastoff !"

Up and up they
started to fly,
over the houses
and into the sky.

The higher they went the
more they were sure,
the stars had gone missing
and the moon was no more.

"Oh no, what do we do now?!"
Henry pressed his nose against the window.

"We go out and look for them."
Elsa said decisively.

"Time to get our space suits on."

They looked to their left,
looked to their right
floated upside down with
not a single star in sight,

Until...

"Oi!"
Something shouted
at Henry.

"Watch where you're going!"

"Sorry!"
Jumped Henry.

"Oi!"

"Who said that?!"
Elsa asked, looking around.

"I did!"
Two eyes opened and glared at Henry and Elsa.

"Hang on a minute ?!"
Elsa gasped.
"You're a star!"

The eyes rolled at Elsa.
"*Obviously*."
He tutted.

"Why aren't you shining?" Henry blurted out.

"That's rude!" The star snapped at Henry.

"But if you *must* know, it's not *my* fault. Why
don't you ask the moaning moon over there.
They're the one who turned all the lights off!"

So off they went, floating in space.

They bumped and bounced like bumper cars, across the sky of grumbling stars.

Each one pointed to the place, you'd usually see a big moon face.

But there was nothing.

Then they heard a snoring
sound. So they went closer and
finally found the moon!

"Hello?" Henry called out.

The moon opened one eye.

"Go away."

She said and closed her eyes again.

"That's not very nice."
Elsa said.
"We've just come to help."

"It's not me that needs help, it's her."
The moon looked sideways at her other eye
and the stars around her groaned.

"Um, who needs help? There's no one else
here." Elsa asked, very confused.

"Typical! She means me."
Another voice said from the other side of the moon.

"Wow. Are there two of you?"
Elsa tried to float around to see.

"Everyone knows there are two sides to us."
The moon sighed.

"Oh. We just thought you were one moon."
Henry said, instantly regretting it.

here we
go
again...

"Well of course you didn't know I was here! She won't let me shine!"
The moon moaned.

"Fibber! You won't let ME shine!"
The moon shouted back.

"I tried to shine earlier and you stole the light off me."
The moons voice was getting louder and higher.

Watch out everyone!

"YOU! stole it off ME!"
She raised her voice higher.

"BECAUSE IT'S MY TURN."
The moon moaned.

"THAT'S NOT TRUE, IT'S MY TURN."
She moaned back.

"NO, YOU HAD YOUR TURN LAST NIGHT!"

"FIBBER! THE STARS WILL BACK ME UP!"

But the stars were shaking their heads and backing away.

"Um, guys?" Elsa tried to step in.

well
done

"What's happened?" Elsa asked quietly.

"Same as before. She's broken the shine."

"No I didn't, you did."

"I'm sleepy." Henry yawned.

"I'm not surprised."

"It's passed your bedtime."

"But I can't sleep without you and
the stars shining." Henry said.

"Oh."
"Oh."
The moon said together.

meow

"Buzz? what are you doing here?"

"Right. We need to go to bed and we need to get Buzz back before mummy notices." Elsa said decisively.

"But how will I sleep without you all shining?" Henry sighed.

"I'm sorry." The moon said. "I'm trying to shine right now but I can't do it."

"It's hard to get it back when it happens. We get tired."

"I'm sorry. Me too."

"Well, do you have to shine all on your own? Could you maybe help each other?"
Elsa asked.

"But we've always shone one side each, on our own. I'm not even sure how we would help each other..."

"Mummy makes us help each other all the time." Henry said. "It's easy!"

"It is and we're here to help! Now think bright thoughts together and try and share !
Elsa said.

"OK I'm doing it, bright thoughts..."

"Me too! Bright thoughts, bright thoughts!"

The stars were celebrating but the moon saw how tired Henry was and shushed them all. She then gently wafted Elsa, Henry and Buzz towards their rocket with a smile.

Henry yawned and waved and waved and yawned.

The moon quietly promised to keep shining and the stars twinkled happily.

"Goodnight children. We'll be waving each night to you."

"Bye!"

Elsa waved and then made sure everyone got back inside the rocket safely.

"Good night, shine bright." Elsa yawned quietly.

Inside the rocket, Elsa whispered the checks to herself.
"Engine ready."

"Seatbelts on."
She turned around to check Henry and Buzz but they were both already snoring.

"Home time."
Elsa smiled and pressed "GO."

"Is Henry asleep yet?"
Mummy called
upstairs.

"He's in with Elsa."
Daddy said with a laugh.

"They're all fast
asleep in there."

Daddy scooped Henry up and took
him back into his own room and
scooted Buzz off Elsa's head.

Mummy joined daddy
in Henry's room.

"I wonder what he's
dreaming about."

"Superhero's or dinosaurs."
Daddy said. He was right too.

NIGHT NIGHT

X

Printed in Great Britain
by Amazon